THE BABY CHIPMUNK

by Dr. Frances R. Horwich

and Reinald Werrenrath, Jr.

Illustrations by William Neebe

RAND McNALLY & COMPANY · Chicago

Why THE BABY CHIPMUNK was written . . .

Here is a story that will stimulate the children's interest in nature and the natural things around them.

We hope your child will enjoy the experiences of a baby chipmunk as he discovers the world about him.

Miss Frances

A CHIPMUNK is a little animal that you might see almost anywhere outdoors in the country. He is small and brown, and he has black and white stripes on his back. When he wants to, he can move very fast. He moves almost as fast as you can blink your eye.

Once there was a family of chipmunks that lived in a hole in the stump of a tree. There

was a mother chipmunk and a father chipmunk and a baby chipmunk. The baby chipmunk was allowed to play outside in front of
the hole in the stump of the tree, and he liked

to jump onto a log near the stump and
scamper up and down.

Now, chipmunks are very curious little ani-
mals. They like to look into things to see what

is inside. They also like to look over things to see what is on the other side.

This baby chipmunk was just as curious as any other chipmunk. One day he scampered

all the way to the end of the log, and there he saw a big rock. It was so big he couldn't see what was on the other side. Being a very curious chipmunk, he jumped onto the rock

and very carefully crept to the top and looked over.

There was a flower garden, and on the other side of the flower garden was a house.

He was very curious, so he jumped off the rock and crept into the flower garden. There were so many flowers he had to zigzag this way and that way around each plant until he came to the other side.

There was some grass. Beyond the grass was a sidewalk, and next to the sidewalk were the steps going up to the house. The baby chipmunk ran over the grass, across the sidewalk, and came to the steps of the house.

He peeked over the top of the first step. There on the step were three peanuts.

He put the peanuts into his mouth and tucked them into his cheeks as chipmunks do

when they want to carry food. He looked
funny with his cheeks puffed out—but how
would you carry three peanuts if you were a
chipmunk?

He ran back zigzag through the flower garden, jumped over the big rock, scampered down the log and into the hole in the stump of the tree.

That day the chipmunk family had peanuts for lunch.

The next day, when the baby chipmunk was out playing in front of the stump of the tree, he decided to look at the house again.

He scampered along the log, jumped onto the rock, and peeked over the top. The house was still there, and the flower garden, too. He jumped down and ran through the flower garden, zigzagging around the plants.

This time, when he came to the grass, he ran right across and over the sidewalk to the steps. He peeked over the top of the first step. But there were no peanuts! Then he climbed up and peeked over the top of the second

step. There, on the second step, were three
peanuts!

He put them into his mouth and tucked
them into his cheeks. He ran down the steps

and across the grass and zigzagged through the flowers. He jumped up over the rock and scampered down the log and into the hole in the stump of the tree.

The very next day, the baby chipmunk
started off as soon as he could. He was be-
ginning to like peanuts very much. When he

got to the house, he climbed up each step and looked carefully—but there were no peanuts. When he got to the top, what do you think he found? There was a big pile of peanuts. It was

right out in the middle of the porch. He tucked as many as he could into each cheek.

Then he went home for father chipmunk and mother chipmunk and brought them back

with him. They each tucked as many peanuts
as they could into their cheeks. They came
back several times and took the peanuts and
stored them away in their hole in the stump of

the tree. You see, chipmunks have to save some of the food they find in the summer so they will have something to eat in the winter.

Just as the baby chipmunk was tucking the last peanut into his cheek, and his face was puffed up more than it had ever been, he heard a noise! It was someone laughing. And a voice said, "Look, Mother! They took them all!"

And father chipmunk and mother chipmunk and the curious baby chipmunk all ran down the steps and zigzagged through the flowers and jumped up over the rock and

scampered down the log and into the hole in
the stump of the tree.

They had enough food to last them all
winter long.

Who do you suppose put those peanuts there? Did you?